THE STORY OF A MIRROR

Ali Bahrampour

Farrar Straus Giroux • New York

For Elsa

Distributed in Canada by Douglas & McIntyre Ltd.
Color separations by Chroma Graphics PTE Ltd.
Printed and bound in the United States of America by Berryville Graphics
Designed by Jennifer Crilly
First edition, 2003
1 3 5 7 9 10 8 6 4 2

Library of Congress Cataloging-in-Publication Data
Bahrampour, Ali, 1969–
    Otto, the story of a mirror / Ali Bahrampour.— 1st ed.
       p.   cm.
    Summary: Tired of reflecting the customers at Mr. Topper's Hat Store, Otto
manages to escape and have the adventures he had always dreamed of having.
    ISBN 0-374-27078-3
    [1. Mirrors—Fiction. 2. Voyages and Travels—Fiction.] I. Title.

PZ7.B1425 Ot 2003
[E]—dc21
                                                                    00-64628

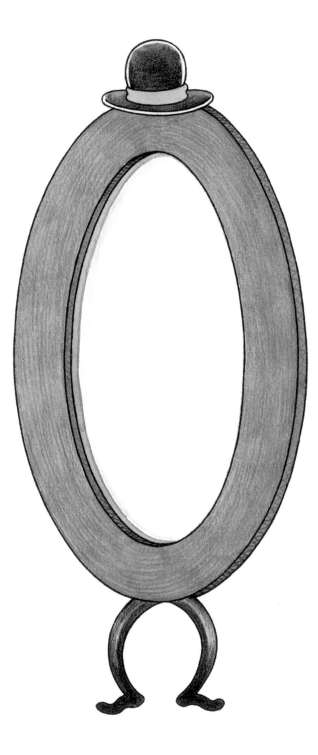

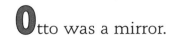tto was a mirror.

He lived and worked at Topper's Hat Store. His job was to stand still and reflect the customers as they tried on hats and looked at themselves. "You look great in this hat!" Mr. Topper would tell them.

Otto found the whole routine extremely boring. Face after face, hat after hat, pose after pose. Boring, boring, boring. It was always with great relief that Otto watched the last customer leave and Mr. Topper lock up the shop and go home.

As soon as Mr. Topper was gone, Otto would clamber into his favorite armchair in the back of the store. There he would read from a pile of old books that Mr. Topper sometimes stood on when he needed to reach a hat on a high shelf. Otto loved to read about faraway lands, plants, and animals—anything about the world beyond the hat store. His secret dream was to travel the globe and reflect all these wonders in person.

Most of all, Otto longed to reflect the beautiful Roodle Tree, which he read about in a book entitled *My Glorious Travels*, by Captain Lemmy. There was only one Roodle Tree in the world, and it grew on the Isle of Koodle. Many's the night Otto fell asleep in his chair dreaming of this fabulous tree.

But in the morning he would wake up and find himself right back at work. Business was good. Hats were selling like crazy. Otto was more bored than ever.

One day he felt so bored . . .

. . . that he decided to have a little fun.

Mr. Topper was horrified. He ran over and scolded Otto, but not for very long, because he felt foolish yelling at his own angry face. He warned Otto never to do anything like that again.

But later that day Otto did do something like that again.

And again and again.

"That does it!" said Mr. Topper. Otto had never seen him so furious. Mr. Topper picked him up and hung him on a nail in the back of the shop.

But now Mr. Topper was in a fix. He had customers coming in who would want to see themselves in the mirror. Noticing an empty frame leaning against the wall, Mr. Topper had an idea. He dragged the frame out to the front of the shop and jumped behind it just as a customer strolled in.

But Mr. Topper turned out
to be a disaster as a mirror.

First he lifted the wrong arm.

Then he got so confused he
lifted the wrong limb altogether.

No, he wasn't fooling anyone.

Finally Mr. Topper ran to Otto and begged him to come back to work. "Please!" he cried. "Curly Joe is coming! Curly Joe!"

Curly Joe was Mr. Topper's best customer. He was proud of his beautiful hair, and he loved to buy hats.

Sometimes he would buy a small hat to show off how much hair he had.

Sometimes he would buy a big hat, to tease and tantalize people with just a curl showing.

Today Curly Joe was buying seven hats at once. "I'm going to a *very* important party," he explained to Mr. Topper. Otto suddenly felt like pulling one of his tricks. But he decided to try to hold it in and behave. He tried. He really tried.

But Otto couldn't help it.

"Nobody makes fun of Curly Joe!" Curly Joe screamed. "Mirror," he growled, "I'm going to smash you to bits." He raised his cane to strike.

Otto was terrified. Surely Mr. Topper would stop this madman. But Mr. Topper seemed just as angry and simply muttered, "The customer is always right!"

Otto made a dash for the door.

"Stop that mirror!" Curly Joe and Mr. Topper cried.
Otto ran for his life.

He was frightened and excited. He felt dizzy at all the new sights he was reflecting.

After a frantic chase, Otto found himself cornered.

"This is the end," Otto thought, and he leaned back to reflect the infinite blue sky one last time before he'd be smashed to smithereens. Then something completely unexpected happened.

A large bird looking for shiny objects to decorate her nest with swooped down and scooped Otto up.

How tiny the city looked. Otto spotted Topper's Hat Store and found it hard to believe he was now soaring so high above it.

Meanwhile, the smell of the sea was making the bird hungry. Deciding that right now a meal was more important than nest decoration, she gently dropped Otto into an empty rowboat and flew off in search of fish.

For days and days the mirror drifted, not knowing where the waves would take him, a little bit scared, but happy nonetheless. At last he was having his own adventure, sailing the seas like his hero, Captain Lemmy.

At night he gazed with wonder at the stars, which he had never seen before. For fun, he made up his own constellations, connecting the glowing dots into shapes and patterns.

One day a storm hit, and Otto was almost washed overboard.

The next morning the sea was calm again. The water seemed to go on forever, endless and unbroken. But a few hours later Otto spotted something in the distance. He couldn't believe it.

The Roodle Tree on the Isle of Koodle! Otto leaped onto land and danced a joyous jig. He reflected the Roodle Tree to his heart's delight—the leaves, the branches, the trunk . . . It was more beautiful than in the picture, more colorful than he had ever imagined. But what was this?

Otto was amazed to see another mirror sitting beneath the Roodle Tree. "How did you get here?" he asked her. The mirror told Otto her name was Miranda. She had been the mirror on Captain Lemmy's ship and had escaped just before he set sail from the Isle of Koodle. Now Miranda spent her days making sculptures out of seashells.

The two mirrors immediately hit it off. Otto told Miranda the story of his own escape, about the hat store, Mr. Topper, and Curly Joe. Miranda told Otto how tired she had grown of the pompous Captain Lemmy and the ridiculous way he twiddled his mustache whenever he looked in her.

As the mirrors chatted, they discovered they shared the same dream: to travel around the world and reflect all its marvels. "Say no more!" exclaimed Otto. "Come in the boat with me, Miranda. We'll travel around together."

And so they did. And the two mirrors reflected many wonderful things. But sometimes, on a moonlit night, Otto and Miranda just liked to look at each other, reflecting back and forth, back and forth, on and on and on, forever and ever and ever.